THE UNEXPURGATED ADVENTURES OF SHERLOCK HOLMES

BOOK 7

A GANDER AT THE BLUE CARBUNCLE

by NP Sercombe

The un-edited manuscript originally entitled *The Adventure of the Blue Carbuncle* written by Dr. John Watson and Sir Arthur Conan Doyle

Illustrations by Emily Snape

This novel is entirely a work of fiction. The names, characters and incidents portrayed in it are the work of the author's and illustrator's imaginations. Any resemblance to actual persons, living or dead, events or localities, is entirely coincidental.

Published by EVA BOOKS 2020 – c/o Harry King Films Limited
1&2 The Barn
West Stoke Road
Lavant
n/r Chichester
West Sussex PO18 9AA

Copyright © NP Sercombe 2020

The rights of Nicholas Sercombe to be identified as the author of this work have been asserted in accordance with the Copyright, Designs and Patents Act 1988.

A CIP catalogue record for this book is available from the British Library.

ISBN 978-1-9996961-6-0 (Hardback)

Book layout & Cover design by Clare Brayshaw.

Cover illustration by Emily Snape.

Set in Bruce Old Style.

Prepared and printed by: York Publishing Services Ltd
64 Hallfield Road, Layerthorpe, York YO31 7ZQ

Tel: 01904 431213

Website: www.yps-publishing.co.uk

All rights reserved. No part of this publication may be reproduced, stored in a retrieval system, or transmitted, in any form or by any means; by that we mean electrical, mechanical, photocopying, recording or otherwise, without the prior written permission of the publisher.

This book is sold subject to the condition that it shall not, by way of trade or otherwise, be lent, re-sold, hired out or otherwise circulated without the publisher's prior written consent in any form of binding or cover other than that in which it is published and without similar condition including this condition being imposed on the subsequent purchaser.

THE UNEXPURGATED ADVENTURES OF SHERLOCK HOLMES

Books in the Series:

A BALLS-UP IN BOHEMIA
THE MYSTERIOUS CASE OF MR. GINGERNUTS
THE CASE OF THE RANDY STEPFATHER
MY FIRST PROPER RURAL MURDER
THE ORANGES OF DEATH!
THE MAN WITH THE HAIRY FACE
A GANDER AT THE BLUE CARBUNCLE

Nicholas Sercombe is a writer and producer for film and television. He has been lucky enough to work in comedy for most of the Holocene period with some of the greatest performers and writers. He is most comfortable when reading Conan Doyle and even happier when re-writing these extraordinarily entertaining stories by Dr. John Watson.

Emily Snape is a coffee addicted, London based illustrator, who's work can be found internationally in books, magazines, on the web, television and even buses.

She studied at Central Saint Martins, Bristol and Kingston and is rarely found without a pencil in her hand. She loves sketching in the streets of London and thinks life is too short for matching socks.

For lovers of roast goose at Christmas

A Gander at the Blue Carbuncle

(*published in The Strand in January 1892 as*
THE ADVENTURE OF THE BLUE CARBUNCLE
by Dr. Watson and Arthur Conan Doyle)

I had returned to 221B Baker Street upon the second morning after Christmas 1889, having spent the five days of the festivities away in Norfolk with my widowed mother, my two brothers and two sisters. It had been a very enjoyable reunion at Kettlestone House, the first time at Christmas together since the passing of my father five years before and, more recently, Great Uncle Eric's incarceration in Wandsworth.* What with my professional qualification as a medic and having my own practice "down in London" I was perceived to be the natural head of the family and I played up to the role with great pride. True, there was a certain level of resentment about my perceived success from Jed, who was a peat-cutter, and my younger sister Deborah, who managed a local fleapit – a.k.a. *The Drifting Sands* seaside hotel – but little did they know about my constant struggle against impecuniosity. I was also the eldest child, which gave me natural superiority in the pecking order. None of them had ever heard of *The Strand* magazine, let alone read a copy, so as there was a sniff of envy in the air already I decided not to

---

* see *The Mysterious Case of Mr. Gingernuts*

mention my partnership with the infamous Sherlock Holmes; I didn't wish to stoke the bonfire of jealousy and I intended to keep it that way. On Boxing Day, we had made an excursion *en famille* to the races at the Fakenham meet. I kept my head low, my coat collar high and my hat pulled down tightly on my forehead for fear of being recognised by a loyal *Strand* reader, whose number seemed to be growing with each adventure published. I had backed three winners, making a grand profit of £4. 10/-, which was more than enough to blow the saddlebags off the donkey down at Mother Kelly's that evening. It had, after all, dear adventure enthusiast, been a while since I had been out on the track, so to speak, so when I returned home and walked into the apartment, I felt like one of the horses at the start of a Fakenham race: a ball of pent-up energy, all frothing at the mouth, and ready to fly down to the finish line, and to victory!

I was also anxious to wish my dear friend, Sherlock Holmes, the compliments of the season. He was lounging upon the sofa in a purple dressing-gown, a pipe-rack within his reach upon the right, and a pile of crumpled morning papers, evidently newly studied, near at hand. Beside the couch was a wooden chair, and on the angle of the back hung a very seedy and disreputable hard felt hat, much worse for the wear, and cracked in several places. A lens and a pair of forceps lying nearby suggested that the hat had been suspended in this manner for the purpose of examination.

'You are engaged,' said I. 'Perhaps I interrupt you?'

'Not at all. I am glad to have a friend with whom I can discuss my results. The matter is a perfectly trivial one' (he jerked his thumb in the direction of the old

My friend was more than capable of holding a party on his own, and with himself.

hat), 'but there are points in connection with it which are not entirely devoid of interest, and even instruction.'

I seated myself in his armchair and warmed my hands in front of his crackling fire, for a sharp frost had set into southern England, and the windows were thick with ice crystals. 'I had noticed it, Holmes, and I have no doubt that it is the clue which will guide you in the solution of some mystery, and the punishment of some crime.'

'No, no. No crime,' said Sherlock Holmes, laughing. 'Only one of those whimsical little incidents, which will happen when you have four million human beings all jostling each other within the space of a few square miles. Amid the action and reaction of so dense a swarm of humanity, every possible combination of events may be expected to take place, and many a little problem will be presented which may be striking and bizarre without being criminal. We have already had experience of such.'

'So much so,' I remarked, 'that, of the last six cases which I have added to my notes, three have been entirely free of any legal crime.'

'Precisely. You allude to my attempt to recover the Irene Adler papers, to the singular case of Miss Mary Sutherland, which should have been a crime by the way her stepfather behaved towards her, and to the adventure of the hirsute gentleman of the City of London.'

Ah! The mystery of the man with the hairy face from last summer. That reminded me of what happened immediately afterwards, of me being taken hostage by Professor Moriarty.*

---

* see *The Man with the Hairy Face*

'I may like to add to another crime to that list, Holmes,' I interjected. 'That of my kidnap.'

'I do not recall a client's instruction of that type. No, there are no others, Watson. Now, listen to this…'

I suppose that my capture by Professor Moriarty had hardly seemed like a crime to Sherlock Holmes because he was not acting as a consultant detective; instead he was on an involuntary mission to secure my release. Actually, whilst he was gone, my time with the Professor had turned out to be quite a remarkable experience. I haven't written anything about this before now but, on that morning, whilst the great detective had delivered Moriarty's blackmail to the Prime Minister, the Professor had insisted that we spend the morning together as his "hostage" at Mother Kelly's, dining on *Eggs Rossini*. I should explain that *Eggs Rossini* was a novelty service on the *à la carte* Menu of Depravity at Mother Kelly's, recently created by *Madame* herself to encourage business revenues in the mornings. This had come about after the esteemed knocking-shop owner had discovered the gorgeous Signorina Bella Rossini on holiday in Naples and together they had cultivated an unique service: she offered herself to the establishment's clientele as an alternative to the traditional dining table, dressed only in her birthday suit. Mother Kelly's chef laid out the breakfast carefully – shakily – onto her naked olive skin and we had the pleasure of removing each item as we desired. The chef then made a hasty exit and the Professor and I did the washing up, so to speak. I was his guest and what a charming host he was! And Bella was a most extraordinary talent – an instant success with the locals and was booked up for weeks in advance. She was a credit to her pro…

'WATSON!'

'Yes, Holmes? Sorry, I became distracted.'

'Stop daydreaming! Now, have you ever come across a local commissionaire called Peterson?'

'Yes.'

'It is to him that this trophy belongs.' Holmes pointed once again to the disreputable hat.

'That is his?'

'No, no; he found it. Its owner is unknown. I beg that you will look upon it, not as a battered billycock, but as an intellectual problem. And, first, as to how it came here. It arrived upon Christmas morning, in company with a good fat goose, which is, I have no doubt, roasting at this moment in front of Peterson's fire. The facts are these…'

'Please, Holmes,' said I, rising from the chair, 'may I find myself some refreshment first?' I should have known, dear reader, should I not that the great detective would have a new puzzle for his sounding-board to absorb and grabbed a glass before saying "good morning?"'

'Please, Doctor, help yourself. You will find an excellent amontillado from Inglesias family; Senor Julio of *The George and Vulture* celebrates the Season annually in fine style.'

'Which is a strange gift when one thinks about it, Holmes, because I was under the impression that Inglesias is a Portuguese?'

'Indeed, he is, Watson, but you are trying to be too clever. The family has relations by marriage in Jerez. Now, please, sit down and listen.'

Oh, how Sherlock Holmes loved to tell a story. Thank goodness for that, because here we are now in my seventh written account of such extraordinary events. I whisked myself into position back in the armchair and grinned at my friend. 'I am all ears, Sherlock.'

Holmes sighed tetchily and then picked up from where had left off. 'As I was saying, at about four o' clock on Christmas morning, Peterson, who, as you know, is a very honest fellow, was returning from some small jollification, and was making his way homewards down the Tottenham Court Road. In front of him he saw, in the gaslight, a tallish man, walking with a slight stagger, and carrying a white goose that was very much alive, in a sling. As he reached the corner of Goodge Street a row broke out between this stranger and a little knot of roughs. One of the latter knocked off the man's hat, on which he raised his stick to defend himself, and, swinging it over his head, smashed the shop window behind him. Peterson had rushed forward to protect the stranger from his assailants, but the man, shocked at having broken the window and seeing an official-looking person in uniform rushing towards him, dropped the goose, took to his heels, and vanished amid the labyrinth of small streets which lie at the back of Tottenham Court Road. The roughs had also fled at the appearance of Peterson, so that he was left in possession of the field of battle, and also of the spoils of victory in the shape of this battered hat and a most unimpeachable Christmas goose.'

'Which surely he restored to their owner?'

'My dear fellow, there lies the problem. It is true that 'For Mrs. Henry Baker" was printed upon a small card, which was tied to the bird's left leg, and it is also true that the initials "H.B." are legible upon the lining of this hat; but, as there are some thousands of Bakers, and some hundreds of Henry Bakers in this city of ours, it is not easy to restore lost property to any of them. As for the goose himself, he refused to answer any of Peterson's questions.'

'Ha-ha, Holmes! So, what, then, did Peterson do?'

'He brought round both hat and goose to me on Christmas morning, knowing that even the smallest problems are of interest to me.'

'Hence we are nearly always penniless...'

'Don't interrupt, Watson! Now, this goose Peterson took back home with him was alive and wrapped into a sling and is probably still retained until this very morning. Its finder has carried it off therefore to fulfil the ultimate destiny of a goose, whilst I continue to retain the hat of the unknown gentleman who lost his Christmas dinner.'

'Did he not advertise?'

'No.'

'Then, what clue could you have as to his identity?'

'Only as much as we can deduce.'

'From his hat?'

'Precisely.'

'But you are joking. What can you gather from this battered felt?'

'Here is my lens. You know my methods. What can you gather yourself as to the individuality of the man who has worn this article?'

I took the tattered object in my hands and turned it over rather ruefully. It was a very ordinary black hat of the usual round shape, hard and much the worse for wear. The lining had been of red silk, but was a good deal discoloured; the initials 'H.B.' were scrawled upon one side. It was pierced in the brim of the hat-securer, but the elastic was missing. For the rest, it was cracked, exceedingly dusty, and spotted in several places, although there seemed to have been some attempt to hide the discoloured patches by smearing with ink.

'I can see nothing,' said I, handing it back to my friend. No sooner had I declared this submission than I regretted it! Dammit, I knew, by now, that an offer from the great detective to analyse any event, person or object was the preface to him showing off his skills by pouring out a stream of humiliating facts and insight over the foolish victim unwise enough not to offer some deductions. The fact that they were completely disguised to any normal human being was irrelevant.

'On the contrary, Watson, you can see everything.'

Once again, I was about to become Sherlock Holmes's sounding-board; the teacher educating the pupil in the art of deduction. But I took comfort in the knowledge that he liked to address his thoughts upon a mystery to me, thus experimenting with his theories. I was very good at giving him reactions, which helped him to expound those theories. So, I liked to think that he needed me, maybe not essentially, but as his favourite adjustable spanner in his toolbox. First of all, though, he liked to dish out some humiliation from his lofty position of superior intellect.

'You fail to reason from what you see. You are too timid in drawing your inferences.'

'Then pray, tell me what it is that you can infer from this knackered old hat?'

I threw it over to him. He caught it whilst looking away, completely by natural reaction, like the Doctor himself in the slips.* He gazed at it in the peculiar introspective fashion which was characteristic of him. 'It is perhaps less suggestive than it might have been,' he remarked, 'and yet there are a few inferences which are very distinct, and a few others which represent at least a strong balance of probability. That the man was highly intellectual is of course obvious upon the face of it, and also that he was fairly well-to-do within the last three years, although he has now fallen upon evil days. He had foresight, but has less now than formerly, pointing to a moral retrogression, which, when taken with the decline of his fortunes, seems to indicate some evil influence, probably drink, at work upon him. This may account also for the obvious fact that his wife has ceased to love him.'

'My dear Holmes!'

'He has, however, retained some degree of self-respect,' he continued, disregarding my remonstrance, as usual. 'He is a man who leads a sedentary life, goes out little, is out of training entirely, is middle-aged, has grizzled hair which he has had cut in the last few days, and which he anoints with lime-cream. There are the more patent facts which are to be deduced from his hat. Also, by the way, that it is extremely improbable that he has gas laid on in his home.'

'You are certainly joking, Holmes!' cried I, and found myself clapping my hands together like a circus sea lion. 'This is the most outrageous deduction of an object I have ever heard!'

---

* the legendary cricketer, WG Grace

'Not in the least, Doctor,' said he. 'Is it possible that even now, after I have given you these results, that you are unable to see how they have been attained?'

'I realise, Holmes, that I am very stupid; but I must confess that I am unable to follow you. For example, how did you deduce that this man was intellectual?'

For his answer, Holmes clapped the hat upon his head. It came right over the forehead and settled upon the bridge of his nose. 'It is a question of cubic capacity,' said he: 'a man with so large a brain must have something in it.'

'The decline of his fortunes, then?'

'This hat is three years old. These flat brims curled at the edge came in then.'

'So speaks the James Lock of Marylebone.'

'Oh ha, ha, Watson. Just dampen your sarcasm a moment by looking more carefully. It may not be a hat of St. James's Street pedigree, but it is a hat of very good quality. Look at the band of ribbed silk, and the excellent lining. If this man could afford to buy so expensive a hat three years ago, and has had no hat since, then he has assuredly gone down in the world.'

'Well, it is clear enough, certainly. Better than your theorem that a large head denotes a large brain and, therefore, an intellectual owner. For all that we know, he may be Frankenstein's monster.'

'That may be possible, Watson, especially if fiction were ever to become a reality, but until then we work on facts and truths and feasibilities.'

'Booooring! How about the foresight you declare this gentleman to have, Holmes? And the moral retrogression?'

Sherlock Holmes laughed. 'Here is the foresight,' said he, putting his finger upon the little disc and loop of the hat-securer. 'They are never sold upon hats. If this man ordered one, it is a sign of a certain amount of foresight, since he went out of his way to take this precaution against the wind. But since we see that he has broken the elastic, and has not troubled to replace it, it is obvious that he has less foresight now than formerly, which is a distinct proof of a weakening nature. On the other hand, he was endeavoured to conceal some of these stains upon the felt by daubing them with ink, which is a sign that he not entirely lost his self-respect.'

'Your reasoning is certainly plausible.'

'And feasible, Watson. The further points, that he is middle-aged, his hair is grizzled, that it has been recently cut, and that he uses lime-cream, are all to be gathered from a close examination of the lower part of the lining. The lens discloses a large number of hair-ends, clean cut by scissors of the barber.'

'As only the "Golden Scissors of Soho" would know, eh Holmes?'*

Holmes stared at me and sighed. 'You really did have a jolly Christmas with your family, Doctor! Now, if you please will let me finish off? There is a distinct odour of lime-cream. This dust, you will observe, is not the gritty, grey dust of the street, but the fluffy brown dust of the house, showing that it has been hung up indoors most of the time; while the marks of moisture upon the inside are proof positive that the wearer perspired very freely, and could, therefore, hardly be in the best of training.'

---

* see *The Man with the Hairy Face*

'With all of those attributes that you list, plus the fact that he has a large head says to me that he is a fat...' And I stopped myself suddenly as a memory of Holmes's mother flashed up in my mind. Do you remember that she is about the size of the Albert Hall?* 'It says to me, Holmes, that he is a large man. Heavy-boned.'

'Your facts are sound, and your deduction is highly likely.'

'But what of his wife? You said that she had ceased to love him.'

'This hat has not been brushed for weeks. When I see you, my dear Watson, with a week's accumulation of dust upon your hat, as I do most days, I know that you are not married to Mark any longer.'

'Holmes! My wife's name was Mary.'

'Until the honeymoon, Watson, when she became Mark.' He leaned forwards with the widest of grins on his handsome mug and snapped his fingers in front of me. 'Ha! He had a hidden A-GEN-DER!'**

'How unbelievably amusing of you, Holmes! Did it take you the whole of Christmas to conjure up that vaudeville joke?'

'No, just a moment. It is called wit, Watson. Wit!'

I gasped in resignation – I hardly needed reminding of my wayward marriage – and Holmes noticed my despair. He changed his tone.

'I am sorry, old friend. Sometimes the old wounds take longer to heal.

'Just like your old jokes?'

---

* see *The Case of the Randy Stepfather*

** see *A Balls-Up in Bohemia*

'Touché, mon ami...' said he, leaning back and chuckling Gaulishly.

'Well, you have been very ingenious, Holmes,' said I, now perked up and laughing with him; 'but since, as you said just now, there has been no crime committed, and no harm done save the loss of a goose, all this seems to be rather a waste of energy.'

Sherlock Holmes had opened his mouth to reply when there was a commotion outside the room. We strained our ears. The landing floorboards were taking a hell of a pounding as someone of bulk ran along it and we could hear there was a ship's foghorn sounding off repeatedly, and I quote: "Onk! Onk! Onk! Onk! Onk!, which was interspersed with a man shouting. Suddenly, the door flew open! Peterson the commissionaire rushed into the room with flushed cheeks and the face of a man who is crazed with fear.

'THE GOOSE! THE GOOSE HAS GOT LOOSE, SIR!' he shouted.

We could still hear: Onk! Onk! Onk! and it was getting louder.

'Eh? What of it, then?' remarked Holmes, now standing up quickly.

ONK! ONK! ONK!

'WATCH OUT!' And that was all Peterson had time to say before an enormous great gander ran into the room at top speed, flapping his wings, sticking his head out on his long, thick neck, clacking his sharp yellow beak and hissing and honking. The bird was running amok! Totally berserk! And my goodness, he was a formidable creature! In an instant, the tranquillity of the apartment became mayhem; the

The commissionaire was in a panic about being well and truly goosed!

gander chasing Peterson the commissionaire into the corner – who wedged himself between the Bellangé magazine rack and Auntie Bortzoy's gimcrack card table – then dancing around, flapping his wings some more, eyeing up his quarry and hissing.

Onk! Onk! Onk!

Then, he attacked! Lunging forwards, he buried his bright yellow beak into his victim's rather *grand derrière*! Peterson leaped into the air and screamed:

"MERCY!' he screamed, like a thwarted playground bully. 'GET THE DAMMED THING OFF OF ME!'

Onk! Onk! Onk!

'Watson, for goodness sakes, help the poor man!'

'But Holmes, I have no experience of controlling angry geese.'

'For heaven's sakes, Doctor, WHY NOT?!'

Onk! Onk! Onk!

'GET IT OFF!' Peterson kept on repeating, but the gander was stubborn disobedience itself and, unluckily for him, his screams seemed to enforce the bird's anger, pulling harder on the seat of his trousers and the loose flesh contained therein. Then, he put himself into reverse gear, pulling with all his might, the fat commissionaire going with him, like a tiny tug-boat guiding the *SS Great Britain* into dock. It was, dear reader, a very amusing sight – even Sherlock Holmes was laughing!

'FOR GOD'S SAKES, KILL IT! KILL IT!' screamed Peterson, but all the bird did was honk and find even more strength in its resolve.

'I have an idea which may save us, Holmes,' said I, and dashed for the Napoleon escritoire, pulling the front drawer open upon arrival and grasping the 0.577 Holland revolver. As I brought it up to attention, aiming it in the general direction of the *melée* and giving it a very firm grip with both hands, I could hear Sherlock Holmes shouting out: 'Watson, NO! NOT the Manstopper! DO NOT FIRE THAT GUN IN HERE!' But, luckily, before I could even begin to weigh up the consequences of letting loose this cannon of a gun for the second time in my life, Mrs. Hudson strode into the room and stopped dead in front of us. She placed her hands on her hips – one of them holding a copy of *The Sporting Life* – and she surveyed the situation with her powder-blue eyes, which she flicked at me with a familiar you-are-behind-with-the-rent glare. Dash it! Yet again I would have no choice but to succumb to her demands upon my you-know-what.

'I know how to deal with feral poultry, I do,' said our valiant landlady. 'Put that ludicrous gun down, Doctor, before you make us all have a seizure. And fetch that highland claymore over there.'

Whilst Mrs. Hudson fixed her gaze upon the gander, I replaced the remarkably powerful revolver into the drawer and marched over to the Caledonian Corner of the apartment where my father's legacies were on display. I drew the fancy sword from its McTavish scabbard and looked over to Mrs Hudson.

'Move in slowly, Doctor…' said she, whilst walking cat-footed towards our white-feathered friend, the rolled-up newspaper now presented as an improvised shepherd's crook. 'And show it the sword. Show it you mean business.'

And, sure enough, the goose took notice. This bird was no dimwit. As soon as he caught sight of us from the corner of his eye, he released Peterson's *gluteus horriblis* and squared up to his new foes. It soon became obvious he was confused as to who he should defend himself from first. He flicked his eyes from me to Mrs. Hudson and back.

'I say, Watson, what we have here is a remarkably intelligent animal,' said Holmes, pacing up and down in front of him at a respectable distance, making a detailed study. 'A gander of the highest quality and an unusual specimen. Note the barbed tail, a marking only found occasionally in this species.'

'Move to one side, please, Mr. Holmes,' said Mrs. Hudson, 'whilst I distract the beast. Otherwise Doctor Watson will not have an open view of its neck to lop his head off.'

'I beg your pardon, Mrs. Hudson!' protested I. "Lop his head off?" You want *me* to *execute* this bird?!'

The gander heard me – I told you he was bright – and he swivelled around on his feet to square up to me. He stuck his neck out, lowered his head and hissed.

'Yes, I do, John,' she whispered. 'Are you ready?'

'No, Mrs. Hudson, I simply must protest!' cried Holmes. 'Decapitating such a large bird would spurt blood all over my Azerbaijani prayer mat.'

'Yes, that would be sacrilege, Holmes! That carpet has only ever had human decapitations on it.'

'Oh, for pity's sakes!' she despaired. 'I am in league with a pair of Boy Scouts!' She dashed forward, raising her arm to smite the gander unconscious with *The Sporting Life*, but before she could reach the beast he went into a terrible flapping frenzy and honked repeatedly, more in distress than in anger. She stopped in her tracks and stared, as did we all Then, all of a sudden, the gander arched his back rigid, sending his head bolt upright, extending his neck to full length before leaning violently to one side, going into a spasm and climaxing... before falling onto the Azerbaijani. He was dead, I was sure of it. Holmes was aghast, his jaw dropping at the puddle of saliva that was now forming on his mat.

'Oh well, Holmes,' said I, 'at least he didn't bleed all over it.'

But Holmes said nothing, his gaze fixed upon the convulsing bird. He moved to one side and grasped Mrs. Hudson's arm. She, too, was hypnotised by the gander. I looked down and I saw the reason why: his yellow beak had opened wide, and with a wheezing cough, he expectorated a shiny, azure-blue egg onto the floor, which rolled off the Azerbaijani and stopped by Mrs. Hudson's boot. We simply gawped in bewilderment! We did not know what to make of this extraordinary development! It was Peterson the commissionaire who moved first, picking the egg up in his pudgy hand, studying it and then getting terribly excited.

'See! See this, Mr. Holmes! This is no egg; this is a stone,' he cried, holding it up triumphantly.

Holmes marched forward and took it. 'It is indeed a stone. In fact, it is a jewel stone.' He held out his hand and displayed upon the centre of the palm a brilliantly scintillating blue stone, rather smaller than a bean in size, but of such purity and radiance that it twinkled like an electric point in the dark hollow of his hand. Sherlock Holmes made a whistle, the first time I had ever heard him make such nasty noise. 'By Jove, Peterson!' he remarked. 'This is a treasure trove indeed. I suppose you know what you have got here?'

'Is it a diamond, sir? Maybe a precious stone that cuts through glass, as if it were putty?'

'Wouldn't soft butter be a better comparison?' added Mrs. Hudson.

'Er, yes, of course it certainly would, ma'am,' said Peterson, touching his forelock with respect.

'This is more than a precious stone,' Holmes interjected, before I could offer up moussed-jelly as an alternative to putty and soft butter. 'It is THE precious stone!'

'Not the Countess of Mordor's blue carbuncle!' I ejaculated, causing a moment of open-mouthed amazement from my companions.

'Goodness me, Doctor...YES!' cried Holmes. 'I believe this to the very same jewel. I ought to know its size and shape, seeing I have read the advertisement about it in *The Times* every day lately. It is absolutely unique, and it's value can only be conjectured, but the reward offered of £1,000 cannot be within one twentieth of the market price.'

'A thousand pounds!' remarked the commissionaire. 'Great Lord of mercy!' And he subsided down into a chair and stared from one to the other of us. I found myself doing the same. Firstly, I looked over to Holmes whose face was lit up like the Christmas tree. Then, I diverted to Peterson, who was flabbergasted. Finally, to Mrs. Hudson, who winked and pursed her lips at me with the words "I want you" and tilted her head down towards her ground floor apartment. Hmmm!

'That is the reward,' said Holmes, 'and I have reason to know that there are sentimental considerations in the background which would induce the Countess to

"The goose that laid the golden egg?" No!
It was "the goose that puked the blue carbuncle!"

part with half of her fortune if she could but recover the gem.'

Oh, really?

'I say, Holmes,' said I, 'couldn't we just sell the jewel to one of those professional fences who you know down by the docks and...'

'NO, DOCTOR! No, we couldn't!' barked Holmes.

Mrs. Hudson squeaked a muffled laugh at the great detective's outburst and smiled at me.

'Of course not, Holmes. Only joking...'

'Watson! This is a famous jewel, almost infamous right at this very moment because it was stolen from the Hotel Cosmopolitan. It was only five days ago, on the twenty-second of December, to be precise, that Mr. Jack Horner, a plumber, was accused of having abstracted it from the lady's jewel-case. The evidence against him was so strong that the case has been referred to the Assizes. I have some account of the matter here, I believe.' He rummaged amid his newspapers, glancing over the dates, until, at last, he smoothed one out, doubled it over, and read the following paragraph:

'"Hotel Cosmopolitan Jewel Robbery. Jack Horner, 26, a plumber, was brought up upon the charge of having upon the 22nd inst., abstracted from the jewel-case of the Countess of Mordor the valuable gem known as The Blue Carbuncle."'

'It's funny, you reading that gives me an awful feeling of *déjà vu!*' I quipped, holding my chin like Holmes in mock pontification.

'Shut up, Watson!' Mrs. Hudson giggled again, this time holding her hand up to her mouth in a coquettish style, which I found rather attractive. I got the distinct impression that after a long, Christmas holiday she too was keen to blow the saddlebags off the donkey, so maybe on this occasion we would be good for each other?

'I shall continue, if you two will grace me with your finest manners... "Mr. James Trull, upper-attendant at the hotel, gave his evidence to the effect that he had shown Horner up to the dressing-room of the Countess of Mordor upon the day of the robbery, in order that he might solder the second bar of the grate, which was loose. On returning he found that Horner had disappeared, that the bureau had been forced open, and that the small morocco casket in which, as it afterwards transpired, the Countess was accustomed to keep her jewel, was lying empty upon the dressing-table. Trull instantly gave the alarm, and Horner was arrested the same evening; but the stone could not be found either upon his person or in his rooms. Catherine Cusack, maid to the Countess, deposed to have heard Trull's pathetic cry of dismay on discovering the robbery, and to have rushed into the room, where she found matters were as described by the last witness. Inspector Bradstreet, B division, gave evidence as to the arrest of Horner, who struggled frantically, and protested his innocence in the strongest terms. Evidence of a previous conviction for robbery having been given against the prisoner, the magistrate refused to deal summarily with the offence, but referred it to the Assizes. Horner, who had shown signs of intense emotion during the proceedings, fainted away at the conclusion, and was carried out of the room."'

'What about this James Trull character. He sounds like a rum sort of fellow, especially with a name like that. Surely he must be a suspect?'

'Very good, Doctor!' remarked Holmes. 'Ten out of ten for effort. But no, he is irrelevant. What takes priority now is to establish the sequence of events leading from a rifled jewel-case at one end to the crop of the goose in Tottenham Court Road at the other. You see, Watson, our little deductions have suddenly assumed a much more important and less innocent aspect. Here is the stone; the stone came from the goose, and the goose came from Mr. Henry Baker, the gentleman with the bad hat and all the other characteristics with which I have bored you. So now we must set ourselves very seriously to finding the gentleman and ascertaining what part he has played in this little mystery. To do this, we must try the simplest means first, and these lie undoubtedly in an advertisement in all the evening papers. If this fails, I shall have recourse to other methods.'

'What will you say?'

'Give me a pencil, and that slip of paper. Now, then: "Found at the corner of Goodge Street, a goose and a black felt hat. Mr. Henry Baker can have the same by applying at 6.30 this evening at 221B Baker Street." That is clear and concise.'

'Very, but will he see it?'

'Well, he is sure to keep an eye on the papers, since, to a poor man, the loss was a heavy one. He was clearly so scared by his mischance in breaking the window, and by the approach of Peterson, that he thought of nothing but flight; but since then he must have bitterly regretted the impulse which caused him to drop the bird. Then, again, the introduction of his name will cause him to see it, for everyone who knows him will direct his attention to it. Here you are, Peterson, run down to the advertising agency and have this put in the evening papers.'

'I don't think it is a good idea for Peterson to be running anywhere, Holmes…'

'Hoy!' said Peterson, tucking in his shirt and making himself presentable in the aftermath of his assault. 'Are you saying that I am fat?'

'Watson – would that advice of yours be because Peterson here is, in your opinion…fat?'

Oh dear, it was all about his mother again. Let's face it, she was fat. 'Now that is unfair, Holmes,' I said, 'when I have the health of his heart in my best interests.'

Mrs. Hudson looked at me quizzically: 'Are you saying he's a fat cock?'

'No, Mrs. Hudson, I am not saying that!' Goodness me, that woman had only one thing in mind!

Peterson swaggered over to us, all nonchalant-like. 'You Cockneys have a fancy way with your words, Mrs. Hudson, but it doesn't bother me.' And he whisked the scribbled note from my friend's fingers. 'This fat cock knows how to take care of himself, he does. In which papers, sir?'

'In the *Globe, Star, Pall Mall, St. James's Gazette, Evening News, Standard, Echo* and any other that occur to you.'

'Very well, sir. And the stone?'

'Ah yes, I shall keep the stone. Thank you. And, I say, Peterson, just buy a goose on your way home, and leave this one here with me, for we must have one to give to this gentleman when he arrives to claim his hat this evening at 6.30.'

When the commissionaire had gone, Holmes took up the stone and held it against the light. 'It's a bonny thing,' said he. 'Just see how it glints and sparkles.'

'Almost *épatante*,' added I.

'*Si vrai, mon cher Watson*! But maybe not. It hardly dazzles like a diamond but like every good stone it is, of course, a nucleus and focus of crime and they are the devil's pet baits. In the larger and older jewels every facet may stand for a bloody deed. This stone is not twenty years old. It was found in the banks for the Amony Rover in Southern China, and is remarkable in having every characteristic of the carbuncle, save that it is blue, instead of ruby red. In spite of its youth, it has already a sinister history. There have been two murders, a vitriol throwing, a suicide, and several robberies brought about for the sake of this forty-grain weight of crystallised charcoal. Who would think so pretty a toy would be a purveyor to the gallows and the prison? I'll lock it up in my strong-box now.'

'Just give it here,' said Mrs. Hudson, and swiped it from his grasp to then drop it down the front of her dress, into the soft cheeks of her teats. I had a funny feeling that I would be seeing it again soon.

'Watson – we must drop a line to the Countess to say that we have it.'

'Righto, Holmes,' I said, picking up the pen and paper from nearby where the great detective had finished scribbling his advertisement copy. 'Do you think this man Horner is innocent?'

'I cannot tell.'

'Well, then, do you imagine that this other one, Henry Baker, had anything to do with the matter?'

'It is, I think, much more likely that Henry Baker is an absolutely innocent man, who had no idea that the bird which he was carrying was of considerably more value than if it were made of solid gold. That, however, I shall determine by a very simple test, if we have an answer to our advertisement.'

And you can do nothing until then?'

'Nothing.'

Mrs. Hudson turned to face me and raised her eyebrows at me in a very determined stare.

'In that case I shall…I shall leave here and go to my surgery, then make a professional round of my patients. I shall return this evening at the hour you have mentioned, for I should like to see the solution of so tangled a business.'

'Very glad to see you, Watson. You must attend to your flock. We shall dine at seven, shall we not, Mrs. Hudson?'

'You have woodcock, Mr. Holmes. Fresh from the Romney Marshes. Perhaps I should be examining their crops before I give them a roasting. I may find a diamond necklace, or more?'

We laughed politely, during which Mrs. Hudson flashed her eyes towards me by way of a warning signal; I knew then for certain that I wouldn't be leaving Baker Street that afternoon.

'Come with me, Mrs. Hudson,' said I, walking forwards and offering my arm in escort, 'let us leave Sherlock Holmes and this unfortunate bird in peace to solve the mystery of this extraordinary robbery.'

We exited the apartment with me making a fuss of collecting my hat and my coat my medical bag *en-*

route to the landing and closing the door firmly behind us. We descended the staircase at a brisk pace to the front door, opened it, closed it, opened the door to Mrs. Hudson's apartment and slipped in quietly. This was one way of saving a chilly journey to Kingly Street and an even better way of tucking away my racetrack profit of £4. 10/- for a rainy day.

* * *

I had a very busy afternoon, what with donkeys and saddlebags being blown off all around Mrs. Hudson's opulent apartment, after which I felt thoroughly worn out. In fact, I thought to myself, as Mrs. Hudson spooned a cup of very sweet tea down my throat and fed me a banana, that I felt completely drained, both mentally and physically. The former was taken in the style of me listening to stories of her life before she arrived at 221B Baker Street, which she told to me during the moments of restoration between bouts of the latter. We had never spent such a long time together in such intimacy – who would have thought that we intrepid mountaineers in the range of life's relationships could have climbed four peaks in just one afternoon? But we did, so when it came close to half-past six, I was still trembling like a leaf and had to be helped to my feet. It was imperative to get dressed in precisely the same way as I had left our apartment earlier on; otherwise, Sherlock Holmes would notice the difference and deduce that I had not been doing my rounds all afternoon. Everything was restored to perfection until she slipped the Blue Carbuncle into my pocket and gave it a farewell pat.

*One banana was hardly an adequate restorative.
I needed the whole bunch!*

'Mrs. Hudson, why do you hand me this infamous jewel? I shall be obliged to explain my possession of The Blue Carbuncle to the greatest investigative mind in the world... and I shall fail miserably! You know that I have no chance of convincing him.'

'Well, John, he is certainly not going to fish it out of my cleavage. That man's heart is so cold I feel that I am coming down with a chill even down here,' said she, raising her eyes to the ceiling and our rooms up above. She opened the apartment door. 'Whereas, you, Doctor Watson, you have more warmth than a Sheffield foundry!' She wrapped her arms around me and gave me an affectionate squeeze. 'You will think of something to tell mister know-it-all and keep our secret safe.' I have to tell you that at that moment I felt something come alive inside me. I felt wanted and, for the first time in my life, I was needed. It was a marvellous feeling. Then, she pushed me out into the hallway.

'And don't think that my fascination dilutes the urgency to pay your rent arrears,' was her farewell advice to me. 'This afternoon was just the interest due on the sum outstanding,' and she held her hand to me. That was one hell of an interest payment! I dug around in my pockets and produced two £1 notes, which I placed into her outstretched palm. It was only when I added a third promise-to-pay that she snapped her hand into a clench. She smiled, in a lingering style to warm my insides, one that told me she was satisfied, that she was a whole woman. Then, she closed the door. Even so, I still had a glow in my heart.

Once I had donned my hat and picked up my medical bag, I slipped out of the front door onto the Baker street pavement. It was there that I had a chance to reflect upon what I had learned from Mrs. Hudson that afternoon, which was a total revelation to me! What a busy life she had led, and she was only thirty-five years old now. She had been born within the sound of Bow bells and brought up in a loving family in East London. No money, of course, but she had a very happy childhood. Then, how at sixteen, she had become a nurse, which was a pioneering profession in 1865 and been be-friended by a certain Mr. Joshua, who was a resident at Sunny Acres, a nursing home where she worked in Golders Green. She told me how he had loaned her the money to buy the land she needed and a derelict property, miles away, down in Knightsbridge, and…

'Excuse me, good sir,' interrupted a very large fellow to my face, 'but would this be number 221B?

I pointed up to the plaque cemented to the architrave above the door and engraving upon the fanlight, which was illuminated by the hallway lights. 'What do you reckon, Mr. Baker?'

The chap was startled that I addressed him so and he clawed the Scotch bonnet from his large, round head in greeting.

'I am sorry,' said he, 'but are we acquainted?' He rapped the knocker on the front door.

'No, sir! But I am able to guide you to somebody who you will wish to be acquainted with.'

Mrs. Hudson opened the door and played up to our subterfuge as well as any Garrick actress. 'Good evening, Doctor Watson' she announced, much louder than usual and throwing her voice up the staircase. She nodded to Mr. Baker. 'I see that you finished your rounds, Doctor. Here – please take the pebble that Mr. Sherlock Holmes gave to me for safe keeping and return it to him.'

She slipped something into my pocket, and I was able to show Mr. Baker, my involuntary witness, up the stairs to our apartment. That didn't stop Mrs. Hudson giving me a cheeky grin and lick of her lips to send me upon my way.

* * *

'Mr. Sherlock Holmes!' announced I, as we walked through the door. I dropped my medical bag by the hat stand and removed my hat and coat whilst our guest marvelled at his first sight of the great detective. I made straight for the fireplace.

'Mr. Henry Baker, I believe,' said Holmes, rising from his armchair and greeting his visitor with the easy air of geniality which he could so readily assume. 'Pray take this chair by the fire. Come on Watson – it is a cold night. Make some room!'

I jumped back out of the chair by the fire and stood by as Mr. Baker descended his large carcase into it.

'I observe, Mr. Baker, that your circulation is better adapted for summer than for winter.'

'Really?' said our rather forlorn-looking guest. But before he was able to enquire further, Sherlock Holmes sprang into action.

'Is that your hat, Mr. Baker?'

'Yes, sir, that is undoubtedly my hat.'

He was a man with rounded shoulders, a massive head (as I predicted and just described), and a broad, intelligent face, sloping down to a pointed beard of grizzled brown. A touch of red in nose and cheeks, with a slight tremor of his extended hand, recalled Holmes's surmise as to his habits. His rusty black frockcoat was buttoned right up in front, with the collar turned up, and his lank wrists protruded from his sleeves without a sign of cuff or shirt. He spoke in a low staccato fashion, choosing his words with care, and gave the impression generally of a man of learning and letters who had had ill-usage at the hands of fortune.

'We have retained these things for some days,' said Holmes, 'because we expected to see an advertisement from you giving your address. I am at a loss to know now why you did not advertise.'

Our visitor gave a rather shamefaced laugh. 'Shillings have not been so plentiful with me as they once were,' he remarked.

In other words, he was skint. Yet another client who couldn't afford to pay us for our services when we needed money urgently for the rent – after all, I could only hold Mrs. Hudson's fixation for so long. But hold on! Maybe we could keep Mum about the jewel and revisit my idea of earlier on. After all, I had it in my jacket pocket.

'Pray, tell us your story Mr. Baker.'

'I had no doubt that the gang of roughs who assaulted me had carried off the bird. I did not care to spend more money in a hopeless attempt at recovering them.'

'Very naturally. By the way, about the bird – we were compelled to eat it.'

'To eat it!' Our visitor half rose from his chair in his excitement.

'Yes, I am afraid so. It would have been no use to anyone had we not done so. But I presume this other goose upon the sideboard, which is about the same weight and perfectly fresh, will answer your purpose equally well.'

What "other goose?" I looked over to the sideboard and there, sure enough, was our irascible gander from earlier on but now he was plucked and tucked, bald as country pastor and ready for the oven. The de-feathering and evisceration had taken place that afternoon, but not by Mrs. Hudson's hand – I could guarantee that – so had it been Holmes who had prepared the bird?

'Oh certainly, certainly!' answered Mr. Baker, with a sigh of relief.

'Of course, we still have the feathers, feet, crop, head and other bits of your own bird, if you so wish to have them.'

The man burst into a hearty laugh. 'They might be useful to me as relics of my adventure,' said he, 'but beyond that I can hardly see what use the *disjecta membra* of my late acquaintance are going to be to me.'

'They would make a nice soup?'

'Shut up, Watson!'

'No sir, I think that, with your permission, I will confirm my attentions solely to the excellent bird which I perceive upon the sideboard.'

Sherlock Holmes glanced sharply across at me with a slight shrug of his shoulders, which I took to be a sign of warning. I decided not to offer any further light-hearted advice.

'There is your hat, then, and there is your bird,' said he. 'By the way, would it bore you to tell me where you got the other geese from? I am somewhat of a fowl fancier, and I have seldom seen a better-grown goose.'

'Certainly, sir,' said Baker, who had risen and tucked his newly gained property under his arm. 'There are a few of us who frequent The Queen's Inn near the Museum – we are to be found in the Museum itself during the day, you understand. This year our good host, Mandelson by name, instituted a goose-club, by which, on consideration of some few pennies every week, we were to receive a bird at Christmas. My pennies were duly paid, and the rest is familiar to you. I am very much indebted to you, sir, for a Scotch bonnet is fitted neither to my years nor my gravity.' With a comical pomposity of manner, he bowed solemnly to both of us and strode off upon his way.

'So much for Mr. Henry Baker,' said Holmes, when he had closed the door behind him. 'It is quite certain that he knows nothing whatever about the matter.'

'Yerrrsss....' said I. 'And nothing whatever about his manners. We restored his hat and his goose to him. He didn't even offer to recompense us, not even for the cost of the advertisements in the papers! Still, I liked the idea of his goose-club in his local pub. Do you think that we could set up the same at Mother Kelly's? A few pence per week for a fine bird each Christmas?'

'It is a scheme that has its merits, Doctor. I presume from the subject-matter of that comment of yours that we are impecunious?'

'Yes, currently, we are poor, but I did manage to pay some of the rent arrears this afternoon.'

'Really? What with?'

Oh, my goodness! I had let the cat slip out of the

bag. 'My good fortune at the Boxing Day Fakenham meet, Holmes?'

'Oh, well done, Watson! I had no idea that you studied the form of steeplechasers.'

That was close. Too close! I didn't want Holmes to know about my arrangement with Mrs. Hudson. I could see that my reference to this afternoon had set him thinking but then, fortunately, he set off on a new tack.

'Are you hungry, Watson?'

'No, not particularly.'

'Good! Then I suggest we turn our dinner into a supper and follow up this clue while it is still hot.'

'By all means.'

It was a bitter night, so we stumbled around by the apartment door dressing up in heavy clothing; drawing on our ulsters, hauling on heavy coats and placing hats and, finally, Holmes insisted we wrap colourful cravats about our throats. By the time we had finished, we would have blended into the ambience of any bar in the North Pole.

* * *

Outside, the stars were shining coldly in a cloudless sky, and the breath of the passers-by blew out into smoke like so many pistol shots. Our footfalls rang out crisply and loudly as we swung through the doctor's quarter (minus yours truly): Wimpole Street, Harley Street, and so through Wigmore Street into Oxford Street, the "bum crack" of London. In a quarter of an hour we were in Bloomsbury at The Queen's Inn, which is a small public-house at the corner of one of the streets which runs down into Holborn. Holmes pushed open the heavily engraved glass door of the saloon bar. We walked over the threshold of the vestibule and a tall, handsome black man drew us to a gentle halt. He gave us a look up and down, his experienced eye taking in our fine clothing.

'May I say, *messieurs*,' said he, in a thick Froggy accent, 'that I admire your cravats. *Très chic!*'

He nodded to himself and offered to take our coats and hats, which we declined because we anticipated our business in the pub to be brief: "a one-pint affair," as Holmes put it. This presented no problem to the doorman, who, all of a sudden, I seemed to recognise.

'I say, are you not Jackie Halliday, the Froggy middleweight champion?'

Holmes threw me a curly-lipped gawp of sarcasm and raised his eyebrows disbelievingly.

'*Mais oui, Monsieur!*' he said, behind a friendly smile, causing Holmes to dislocate his jaw and drop it onto the floor.

'*Le Grenouille-de-Guadelope!*' said I in my finest French.

'*Oui, Monsieur! Vous êtes très gentil! Mais...* it is many years since, *je pense...* I do not deserve to be named *le champion au fin de dix-huit cent quatre-vingt-neuf, non?*

He opened the door to *l'interieur* and we marched in, with Holmes muttering under his breath "I don't believe it, I really don't..." as we reached a ruddy-faced, white-aproned landlord and ordered two glasses of beer. Whilst he was pouring our drinks, Holmes kept giving me sideways glances – it was all about my knowledge of

French colonial boxing and how come *he* didn't know – whilst I looked around the room. There was a lady also keeping the bar who, I have to say, rather caught my eye. She was tall and slim with dark, luscious hair that framed a classical, Grecian face but it was the sheer elegance of her form that made me look in earnest – the tight woollen sweater promoting a marvellous top hamper sitting over a soft leather dress that hem-lined just above the knee, just the right length for showing off her shapely legs. Hmmm...and they looked perfect. She must have felt my gaze upon her (or maybe she heard me growling?) because she turned away from her conversation with a gentleman customer and beamed me a radiant smile. I returned the compliment with a small wave of my fingers.

'Hoy! You!' said the aproned landlord, and he was pointing his finger at me. 'I'd watch your step. That's Jacquie's friend.' He jerked his thumb towards the front vestibule. 'And he's the jealous type.'

'Excuse me, landlord...' said Holmes, 'but how did you spell Jackie?'

'Jacquie, sir.'

'Strange...'

'No, Holmes, he is French.'

But the great detective didn't look convinced. I thanked the man profusely for the warning and turned my shoulder towards the lady barkeep – she was out of sight and out of mind, and I was not going to cause trouble with the champion pugilist. We lifted the glasses of beer, which had the appearance of as fine an ale as one could find anywhere.

'Your beer should be excellent if it as good as your geese,' said Holmes, taking a large swig of beer.

'My geese?' The landlord seemed surprised.

'Yes. I was speaking only half an hour ago to Mr. Henry Baker, who was a member of your goose-club.'

'Oh, that! Yes, we run a number of clubs from The Queen's, sir, but none of them is resident. Those were not *our* geese.'

'Indeed! Whose, then?'

'I get two dozen from a salesman in Covent Garden every year.'

'Indeed! I know some of them. Which was it?'

'Breckinridge is his name.'

'Ah! I don't know him. Well, here's to your good health, landlord, and prosperity to your house. Goodnight.'

'Hold on a moment, Holmes,' said I, grasping my glass by the handle, 'I haven't finished my beer.'

'Yes, I think you should hold on a moment, good sirs...' said the landlord, and he leaned in close, to draw us into his orbit and speak in confidence. 'You seem to be a couple of likely lads. As I just said, we run a number of clubs from this pub. We have a couple of racing days at Cheltenham in March where we all stay in the Cotswolds for the best part of a week. We have the summer weekend trip to Brighton where we book out an entire hotel to ourselves. It's very private, get my drift? And then we have a New Year celebration in here, in The Queen's, invitation only. It's a bit of a draw-the-curtains-lock-in event with dinner and dancing. Get the picture?'

'So, a pleasurable time is had by all, eh landlord?'

'Oh yes, we have a very gay time.'

Well, there was nothing wrong with having a gay time.

'You two look like you might fit in very snugly into our gentleman's' club.'

And it was at this moment that both Holmes and I realised that something was in the air. This – The Queen's Inn – was hardly White's or Boodle's. We looked around us and took in some of the clientele. All were finely dressed and well-groomed men, mostly sitting in pairs, which was unusual, and immersed in quiet and amiable conversations. I glanced at Holmes, who was looking in a different direction to my own; when I noticed his eyes bulge, I followed his line of vision. There, tucked in the corner under candlelight, were two men who had finished their chit-chat and had fallen onto one another. I was a man of the world. I didn't need to see any more. I leaned across to Holmes and whispered into his ear. 'We, my friend, are in a bit of a pickle!'

Holmes leaned in close to me. 'Too right, Watson. This boys' club is an illegal establishment. Even the bar lady over there is a bar gentleman.'

'Hmm. I had spotted that too, Holmes,' I remarked, very matter-of-fact. Blimey, was she?!

'No, you hadn't, Watson. When *will* you learn? Importantly, the management will not wish to be exposed and imprisoned. If they get the merest hint that I am a private detective and, therefore, deemed to a contingent element of law enforcement, we are done for.'

'We must escape, Holmes,' said I, through gritted teeth.

'The only route out of the building is guarded by a champion pugilist. I may have a solid grounding in the noble art of boxing, Watson, and can handle myself competently, but I am not sure if I could take on Jackie Halliday and succeed.'

'It's *Jacquie*, Holmes. And you are correct; *Le Grenouille-de-Guadelope* will beat you up. We are going to exit through the loo window.'

'Just like the Hurlingham Club Christmas ball?'

'Just like the Hurlingham. Landlord! Direct us to the gentleman's lavatory.'

'You two really are eager to get on, aren't you?' I frowned at the rather bizarre reply. 'Down the corridor there and on the left.'

I glanced over to the lady barkeep and I swear she gave me a wink; that girl had a certain something, but I couldn't quite put my finger upon what it was. Holmes and I bustled our way down the passage in a determined and hasty exit.

* * *

'Now for Mr. Breckinridge,' Holmes said, buttoning up his coat, as we came out into the frosty air. 'Remember, Watson, that though we have so homely a thing as a goose at one end of the chain, we have at the other a man who will certainly get seven years' penal servitude unless we can establish his innocence. It is possible that our inquiry may but confirm his guilt; but, in any case, we have a line of investigation that has been missed by the police, and which a singular chance has placed in our hands. Let us follow it out to the bitter end. Faces to the south, Watson, and quick march!

'Yes, quick march indeed, before Jacquie realises that we have dropped out the back.'

After the rather awkward exit from The Queen's Inn, I could understand why Holmes wished to seize the moment and move on without reflection. It is safe to tell you, dear reader, that we had found the location of the lavatory easily enough, but so had many other patrons before us – the place was choc-a-block with clientele. From the moment we entered the room we were being jostled, but when we didn't enter the spirit of the gathering, it soon became a mêlée. We spent no time in delaying our departure! Holmes wrenched open the window and we climbed through as fast as we were able. Both of us struggled to wriggle through the very narrow aperture, hence our coats having to be refitted on the street, and we had endured some high-spirited, rear-guard assistance (of the manual variety) from the clientele during our departure.

We passed across Holborn, down Endell Street, and so through a zigzag of slums to Covent Garden Market. One of the largest stalls bore the name of Breckinridge upon it, and the proprietor, a horsy-looking man, with a sharp face and trim whiskers, was helping a boy to put up the shutters.

'Good evening. It's a cold night,' said Holmes.

The salesman nodded and shot a questioning glance at my companion.

'Sold out of geese, I see,' continued Holmes, pointing at the bare slabs of marble.

'I can let you have five hundred tomorrow morning.'

'That's no good.'

'Well, there are some on the stall with the gas fire.'

'Ah, but I was recommended to you.'

'Who by?'

'The landlord of The Queen's Inn.'

'Were you now?' said the man, giving us a sideways glance with narrow, flinty eyes, an expression that uncovered his knowledge of its men-only clientele. 'I sent him a couple of dozen before Christmas.'

'Fine birds they were, too. Now, where did you get them from?'

To my surprise the question provoked a burst of anger from the salesman.

'Now then, mister…' said he, with his head cocked to one side and his arms akimbo, 'what are you driving at? Let me have it straight, now.'

'It is straight enough. I should like to know who sold you the geese which you supplied to The Queen's.'

'Never a truer word spoken, sir, but I shan't tell you!'

'Oh really?' remarked Holmes, changing his tone completely, and now looking as if he didn't have a care in the world by mooching around carelessly, looking up down and around himself whilst clicking his tongue petulantly. 'Well, I suppose it is a matter of no importance; but I don't know why you should be so het-up over such a trifle.'

That did it.

'HET-UP? You ask me why I am het-up? You'd be more than het-up if you were pestered as I am about my geese! When I pay good money for a good article there should be an end of the business, but no – I keep getting asked "Where are the geese?' and "Who did you sell the geese to?" and "What will you take for the geese?" One would think that they are the only geese in the world to hear the fuss that is made over them. Doesn't anybody realise? I am just the middleman!'

'Well, I have no connection with any other people who have been making inquiries,' said Holmes carelessly. 'If you won't tell us the bet is off, that is all.'

'What bet?'

'I am always ready to back my opinion on a matter of fowls, and I have a fiver on it that the bird I ate is country bred.'

'Well, then, you've lost your fiver! It is town bred!' quipped the salesman in gleeful triumph.

'It is nothing of the kind.'

'I say it is.'

'I don't believe you.'

Mr. Breckinridge reached boiling point and went puce in the face. 'IT RUDDY WELL IS! Do you really think that you know more about fowls than I? You, who have minced your way down here with your moustachioed boyfriend, all the way from The Queen's, can tell me, Stuart Breckinridge, straightest bloke in the Market, who has handled birds since I was a nipper, that those geese I sent to them queens were town bred? Well, sir, you can get stuffed!'

'No, no, no,' continued Holmes, 'I promise you. You are wrong. You will never persuade me to believe they were town bred!'

The man's mouth smarted and his eyes crossed over. My friend had gone too far with his ruse. Breckinridge turned around, marched over to his boy, grabbed the wooden pole that he had been using to operate the shutters, which had a nasty metal hook on the end. He presented it as a threat to the great detective, just like a pikestaff.

'Well, Mr. Cocksure, you know nothing about geese,' challenged he. 'But you have come to the right place for a lesson, m'laddie!'

'I say, Holmes, I think you have a live one here!' said I rather gaily, stating the blindingly obvious. 'Here – you had better defend yourself.'

I had spied a similar shutter-hook on the adjacent stall. It was only one step away and I tossed it over to him. Holmes caught it and adopted what I later found out to be the graceful stance of a Kendo warrior, the shutter-hook now in position as a makeshift sword. Mr. Breckinridge responded by mirroring this ritualistic image, albeit in a more haphazard fashion.

Holmes's face lit up. 'I had no idea that you were a man of honour, Mr. Breckinridge!' said he, inclining his head and bowing from his midriff elegantly. Whilst he was out of Holmes's eyeline, the bewildered salesman looked over at me quizzically – believe me, I had absolutely no idea what Sherlock Holmes was doing – so I responded with a vacant expression and a "don't ask me" gesture. However, I wish I had known more about the Japanese martial arts because what now followed was a complete and utter revelation to me.

Sherlock Holmes descended towards the ground, his legs collapsing steadily underneath him, his head, neck and back absolutely straight as a ramrod. Breckinridge realised that a ceremony was afoot and, in the absence of any insight from yours truly, mimicked Holmes. They acknowledged one other and arose to their full height. Now, Holmes moved forward to within two yards of

Breckinridge. He presented his shutter-hook from the lowest extent of his arms with the point presented upwards – this seemed to be the formal challenge – and the salesman did the same, thus accepting the invitation. Then, the sparring started, the wrought tips of each hazel shutter-hook changing positions – dancing, tapping, threading, like butterflies fighting for the same flower. But this was only foreplay because, all of a sudden Holmes attacked! He leapt forward, screaming, with the speed of a starving snake striking an unsuspecting mouse. In one, flowing, movement Holmes whipped up the shutter-hook above his head and sent it crashing down towards Breckinridge's head. His assailant was startled and may have been flummoxed by the suddenness of the attack but he managed to raise his own shutter-hook above his head, in the perpendicular, and parry the blow. The force of Holmes's strike caused Breckinridge to wobble a second before he responded with a lunge forwards a pace and then a leap into the air. What was this poultry salesman doing? As soon as his feet touched the ground I found out! He held the shutter-hook above his head, like a Heidelberg student displaying a *schlager* on-guard, and then attacked the great detective from above, the wooden sword making a beeline for his head. Holmes defended himself with a series of parries, never getting the chance to thrust back with a responding attack. My goodness, this Breckinridge chap looked skilful! It was only then that the music started up. Breckinridge's boy had pulled out a concertina from nowhere and was playing *The Sailors Hornpipe*. You know the one – diddle-dit doo doo, da-da diddle-diddle dit; diddle it, do-do, da-da diddle-diddle dit; de-de diddle-diddle diddle-diddle diddle-diddle diddle-diddle diddle-diddle

diddle-diddle diddle-dit-dit-dit! Anyway, this changed the mood of the shutter-hook swordfight completely and before you could say hey nonny-no they were into a sabre fight. Then, Breckinridge started to caper, hopping from one foot to the other with a jig-one, kick-one routine, all in-time with the music. Notably, he didn't stop fencing. Suddenly, Holmes went into a spin and threw himself out of the contest.

'I will NOT participate in Morris dancing!' cried Holmes, jumping backwards in a temper and throwing his shutter-hook onto the ground. But Breckinridge took little notice; he just smiled and danced solo with much more vigour, swinging his arms up and down to the rhythm of the music, now thoroughly enjoying himself as the boy put the concertina through its paces.

'I am the Bagman of the North Kent Morris Ring Side,' announced the salesman proudly; and now holding a handkerchief in each hand as he capered. 'Stuart Breckinridge, the Fertility Squire.'

Did that mean he squired the local virgins in some ancient rural ritual? If he did, I might take up Morris dancing as well.

'Is that so, Mr. Breckinridge?' remarked Holmes, now wearing the broadest of smiles. 'I would like to know the location and from whom you bought those Christmas geese and if you refuse to tell me I shall have no choice but to reveal your secret to the National Association of Morris men, for you know as well as I that no Morris man may hold the title of Fertility Squire whilst being the Bagman.'

Breckinridge stopped dancing. The boy closed the concertina. The salesman sank down on his knees in time to the ghastly instrument's last gasps, like a discarded organ bellows at the end of a belter of a hymn. Holmes knew how to get his man!

'All right, Mr Cocksure, I'll tell you what you want to know, but you do play a low-ball game.'

'Believe me, my man, nothing stoops as low as Morris dancing. The name is Sherlock Holmes, not Mr. Cocksure. This is my friend, Dr. John Watson.'

The salesman chuckled to himself and tilted his head side to side. 'Goodness me, who would have thought, eh? Bring me the books, Bill,' said he.

The small boy brought round a small thin volume and great greasy backed one, laying them out together beneath the hanging lamp.

'Now then, Mr. Holmes,' said the salesman, 'I thought that I was out of geese, but before I finish, you will find that there is still one left in my shop. It would give me great pleasure if you would take it away for your supper, gentleman. I have followed your mysteries and adventures in *The Strand* right from the first one, and I am an admirer. Why, to tell the lads that I have danced with the great Sherlock Holmes will be a landmark moment.'

Holmes was crestfallen, his reputation in tatters. Then, the salesman turned wily.

'You see this little book, here? This is the list of the folk from whom I buy my poultry. One sovereign says that my geese are town bred. Do we have a wager?'

Holmes nodded assent as Breckinridge opened the book and displayed the contents to both of us with unerring confidence.

'This page is the country folk, and the numbers after their names are where their accounts are in the big ledger. Now, then! You see this other page in red ink? Well, that is my list of town suppliers. Now, look at that third name. Just read it out to me.'

'Mrs. Oakshott, 117 Brixton Road – 249,' read Holmes.

'Quite so. Now, turn that up in the big ledger.'

Holmes turned to the page indicated. 'Here you are: "Mrs. Oakshott, 117 Brixton Road, egg and poultry supplier."'

'Now, then, what's the last entry?'

'"22nd December. Twenty-four geese at 7 shillings and 6 pence."'

'Quite so. There you are. And underneath?'

'"Sold to Mr. Mandelson, of The Queen's Inn at 12 shillings."'

'What do you have to say for yourself now, Mr. Holmes?'

Sherlock Homes looked deeply chagrined. He drew himself up to his full height and glanced at me. 'Watson. Pay this man a sovereign. No, on second thoughts, make it two. The second one, Mr. Breckinridge, is to buy your silence about our little *contra-temps* that turned into a Morris dance… quite accidentally, of course.'

Then, he turned away with the air of a man whose disgust is too deep for words and set off up the road. I threw half of my Fakenham winnings down upon the slab and the boy, Bill, placed a goose in my arms. I bid the salesman farewell and followed Holmes's footsteps. I found him stopped under a lamp post about fifty yards away from the stall. I joined him and he laughed in the hearty, noiseless fashion which was peculiar to him.

'When you see a man with whiskers of that cut and the "Pink 'un" protruding out of his pocket, you can always bet that he is a bundle of trouble,' said he. 'I dare say that if he had revealed his over-sized handkerchiefs before we engaged in Kendo, I would have guessed that he was a Morris dancer. We would have avoided such a confrontation. As it was, I was tricked. As my grandfather used to say, there are three things that a gentleman should never try out...'

'I know that very saying, Holmes, and we have had a brush with two of them in a single evening.'

'Indeed, Watson! We escaped from each one by a hair's breadth. Even so, it is not without some physical memento. Why, the *gluteus* of my posterior must be a chequerboard of bruises after our fight to escape the Queen's Inn!'

'The same for me, Holmes. They pinched hard. If only the window had opened wider. Maybe we should call it a day and return to Baker Street?'

'Well, my friend, the night is still young. I fancy we are nearing the end of our quest, and the only point which remains to be determined is whether we should go to this Mrs. Oakshott tonight, or whether we should reserve it for tomorrow. It is clear from what that surly fellow said that there are others besides us who are anxious about the matter as well and I should...'

His remarks were suddenly cut short by a loud hubbub, which broke out from the Breckinridge stall. Turning around we saw a little rat-faced fellow standing in the centre of the circle of yellow light which was thrown by the swinging lamp. I thought for a moment that it might be Gripper, the sidekick of Professor Moriarty, but I knew that I was mistaken when he cringed at Breckinridge shaking his fists angrily at him; Gripper would have reacted differently, probably by shooting him dead.

'I've had enough of you and your geese!' he shouted. 'If you come pestering me any more with your silly talk and ridiculous questions I'll set the dog on you. You bring Mrs. Oakshott here and I'll answer her, but what do you have to do with it? Did I buy geese off you?'

'No, but one of them was mine all the same,' whined the little man.

'Well, then, go and ask Mrs. Oakshott for it.'

'She told me to ask you.'

'Well, you can ask the King of Timbuktu, for all I care.'

Is there one?

'I've had enough of you!' he continued. 'Get out of here!' He rushed fiercely forward. The inquirer flitted away into the darkness.

'Ha, this may save us a visit to Brixton Road,' whispered Holmes. 'Come with me, and we will see what is to be made of this fellow.'

Striding through the scattered knots of people who lounged round the flaring stalls, my companion speedily overtook the little man and touched him upon the shoulder. He sprang round, and I could see in the gaslight that every vestige of colour had been driven from his face.

'Who are you, then? What do you want?' he asked in a quavering voice.

'You will excuse me,' said Holmes blandly, 'but I could not help overhearing the questions which you

Holmes just laughed and told me to lose some weight before our next visit to a men-only pub.

put to the salesman just now. I think that I could be of assistance to you.'

'You? Who are you? How could you know anything of the matter?'

'My name is Sherlock Holmes. It is my business to know what other people don't know.'

But you can know anything of this?'

'Excuse me, I know everything of it. You are endeavouring to trace some geese which were sold by Mrs. Oakshott, of Brixton Road, to a salesman named Breckinridge, by him in turn to Mr. Mandelson of The Queen's Inn, and by him to his club, of which Mr. Henry Baker is a member.'

'My word, sir! You are the very man I have longed to meet,' cried the little runt of a fellow, with outstretched hands and quivering fingers. 'I can hardly explain to you how interested I am in the matter.'

Sherlock Holmes hailed a four-wheeler, which was passing by. 'In that case we had better discuss it in a cosy room rather than in this wind-swept market-place,' said he.

The man gave Holmes a sideways glance on the tilt of his cock robin head. 'Somewhere "cosy" eh? You are not regulars at the Queen's Inn, are you dear sirs?' And he flicked his eyes suspiciously in my direction too.

Holmes dithered but then delivered: 'No. The Queen's Inn was part of the enquiry that led us to this place.' The chap seemed to be reassured and smiled. 'Pray, tell me,' said Holmes, 'before we go any further, who is it that I have the pleasure of assisting?'

'My name is John Robinson,' the man answered, with a sidelong glance.

'No, no; the real name, please,' said Holmes sweetly.

'Well, then,' said he, 'my real name is James Ryder.'

'Precisely so. You are the head attendant at the Hotel Cosmopolitan. Pray step into the cab, and I shall soon be able to tell you everything which you would wish to know.'

The little man stood glancing from one to the other of us with half-frightened, half-hopeful eyes, as one who is not sure whether he is on the verge of a windfall or of a catastrophe. Then he stepped into the cab.

* * *

Half an hour later we were back in the sitting room at Baker Street. Nothing had been said during our drive, but the high, thin breathings of our new companion, and the clasping and unclasping of his hands, spoke of the nervous tension within him.

'Here we are!' said Holmes cheerfully, as he opened the door and we filed into the room. 'The fire looks very seasonable in this weather. You look cold, Mr. Ryder. Pray take the basket chair. I will just put on my slippers before we settle this little matter of yours.'

We discarded our coats, hats and scarfs on the rack by the door. I placed the goose on the Serpentine, an occasional table that was more Chippen O'Dale than Chippendale, whilst the great detective swopped his stout leather brogues in favour of some spanking new slippers. These were of a style I had never caught sight of before; well, not outside a theatre. They were quite extraordinary in their design – red satin sides, thin black leather soles, a rather fancy piece of tapestry on the bridge topped with an intricate embroidery that led all the way to the toes and beyond, where lay the *pièce de résistance* of the creation: a long extension of red leather in a curly arrangement turning it into a coil. Holmes noticed my gaping appreciation of his new acquisitions.

'Before you ask, Doctor, if I have been appearing in *Aladdin* at The Palladium or make some pathetic quip about Christmas shopping in Marrakech, I'll have you know that these slippers were a present from an esteemed and grateful client.'

'Aladdin?'

'You couldn't resist, could you?'

'Obviously!'

'The Sultan of Brunei was most grateful for my settlement in the Abode of Peace, namely my consultation with the White Raja over the further annexation of Sarawak.'

'I don't suppose you charged a fee for that service?'

'No. In his community, money is an anathema.'

'Well, then, it is no small wonder that he has so much of it. You are aware that we are still behind on the rent?'

'A mere trifle, Watson, you seem to handle Mrs. Hudson with great sensitivity...'

What did he mean by that? Did he know what I had to offer our landlady in compensation for our late payments? I stared at him intently and, for once, received no inkling of sarcasm. No, I don't think that he did know.

'Now, let us find out if our guest has thawed out. We must not keep him waiting any longer.'

Holmes marched over to the roaring fire, which our fastidious landlady had kept stacked up whilst we were out doing... well, what were we doing? I suppose we had been out drinking and dancing. Now there was something to think about! In just one evening we had gone about our business of detection and investigation in complete innocence, only to find ourselves compromised by patronage of an illegal public house, which was embarrassing, and then caught red-handed participating in a pagan ritual for bearded folk, which was damaging. It was also very painful, on both counts: my posterior was black and blue (from all those men pinching it) and my friend's reputation would be in tatters if Breckinridge blabbed, and the day was not over yet.

'Now, then, Mr. Ryder! You want to know what became of those geese?'

'Yes, sir.'

'Or rather, I fancy of that goose. It was one bird, I imagine, in which you were interested – white with a black bar across the tail.'

Ryder quivered with emotion. 'Oh sir,' he cried, 'can you tell me where it went?'

'It came here.'

'So, it is not that one there?' The little man pointed at my goose on the Serpentine.

'No, certainly not. That is our supper. However, the goose that we both refer to has turned out to be a most remarkable bird. I don't wonder that you should take an interest in it. It laid an egg after it was dead – the bonniest, brightest little blue egg that ever was seen.'

'Some would call it *épatante*, Mr. Ryder,' said I.

'And most would not,' replied my friend blandly, and he threw me a grin. But the start of our interrogation was brought to an abrupt halt as our guest startled us by staggering to his feet and clutching the mantelpiece dramatically with his right hand. Holmes unlocked the strong-box, and held up the blue carbuncle, which shone out like a star, with a cold, brilliant, many-pointed radiance. Ryder stood glaring with a drawn face, uncertain whether to claim or disown it.

'The game's up, Ryder,' said Holmes quickly. 'Hold yourself up, man, or you'll fall into the fire. Watson – give him an arm back into his chair and a dash of brandy. He looks like he has lost all the blood to his feet. Here's a man who hasn't the stomach to go in for felony with impunity.'

I poured some of the Napoleon cognac into a balloon, which he sank in one gulp.

'Now he looks a little more human,' said Holmes. 'What a shrimp he is, to be sure!'

'Steady on Holmes,' I said, 'there's no need to be so abusive.' I studied the fellow in more detail. 'No, on second thoughts, you are correct. Come on, shrimp! What do you have to say for yourself?'

'Yes, Mr. Holmes is quite right. For what I have done, I am that shrimp.'

'I have almost every link in my hands, and all the proofs which I could possibly need, so there is little which you need to tell me. Still, that little may as well be cleared up to make the case complete. You had heard, Ryder, of this little blue stone of the Countess of Mordor's?'

'It was Catherine Cusack who told me of it,' said he, in a crackling voice.

'I see. Her ladyship's waiting maid. Well, the temptation of sudden wealth so easily acquired was too much for you, as it had been for better men before you; but you were not very scrupulous in the means you used. It seems to me, Ryder, that there is the making of a very pretty villain in you. You knew that this man Horner, the plumber, had been concerned in some matter before, and that suspicion would rest the more readily upon him. What did you do, then? You made some small job in my lady's room – you and your confederate Cusack – and you managed that he should be the man sent for. Then, when he had left, you rifled the jewel-case, raised the alarm, and had the unfortunate man arrested. You then...

All of a sudden, Ryder threw himself down upon the rug and clutched at my friend's knees. 'For God's sake, have mercy!' he shrieked. 'Think of my father! Of my mother! It would break their hearts. I never went wrong before! I never will again, I swear it on a Bible. Oh, don't bring it into court! For Christ's sake, don't!'

'Get back into your chair!' said Homes sternly.

"Yes, get back there, you filthy dog!' said I, enjoying hunting in a pack with my companion and shunting my boot up his posterior to push him back into his seat.

'It is very well to cringe and crawl now,' urged Holmes, 'but you thought little enough of this poor Horner in the dock for a crime of which he knew nothing.'

'Yes, poor Jack Horner, sitting in his corner!' I goaded, which was such a pathetic quip that it evoked a look of dismay from the great detective.

*I hadn't kicked another human being since my days in the army.
I made a mental note to try it more often!*

'I will fly, Mr. Holmes! I will leave the country, sir.'

'We don't believe a word of it, you scoundrel!' I bawled at him.

'If I abscond the charge against him will break down.'

Holmes's anger subsided a little. He clasped his chin in his hand. 'Hmmm. We will talk about that. And now let us hear a true account of the next act. How came the stone into the goose, and how the goose came into the open market? Tell us the truth, for there lies your only hope of safety.'

Ryder passed his tongue over his parched lips. 'I will tell you it just as it happened, sir,' said he. 'When Horner had been arrested, it seemed to me that it would be best for me to get away with the stone at once, for I did not know at what moment the police might not take it into their heads to search me and my room.'

'Ha! Fat chance!' said Holmes, spitting out the words.

'Quite so! The police using their brains?' added I, laughing along with Holmes. 'Pray continue, shrimp.'

'Well, gentlemen, there was no place about the hotel where it would be safe. I went out, as if I was on some commission, and I made for my sister's house. She had married a man named Oakshott, and lived in Brixton Road, where she fattened fowls for the market. On the way there every man I met seemed to me to be a policeman or a detective, and for all that it was a cold night, the sweat was pouring down my face before I came to the Brixton Road. My sister asked me what the matter was, and why I was so pale. I made the excuse that I had been upset by the jewel robbery at the hotel.

Then I went into the back yard and smoked a pipe and wondered what it would be best to do.'

'I had a friend once called Maudsley, who went to the bad, and has just been serving his time in Pentonville. One day he had met me and fell into talk about the ways of thieves and how they could get rid of what they stole. I knew that he would be true to me, for I knew one or two things about him, so I made up my mind to go right on to Kilburn, where he lived, and take him into my confidence. He would show me how to turn the stone into money. But how to get him in safety? I thought of the agonies I had gone through in coming from the hotel. I might at any moment be seized by the police and searched, and there would be the stone in my waistcoat pocket. I was leaning against the wall at the time, looking at the geese which were waddling about round my feet, and suddenly an idea came into my head which showed me how I could beat the best detective that ever lived.

'DONT BE RIDICULOUS, MR RYDER!' I shouted out involuntarily, and Holmes and I fell about laughing. 'THAT is impossible!'

'I am sorry?' bleated the shrimp, now cowering back into his chair. 'Have I said something wrong?'

I was about to explain that he was sitting in the presence of the greatest private detective that had ever lived – the only private detective that had ever lived – when that very man himself leaned forward and touched my arm, indicating a need to keep our identities a secret.

'What I mean is this…Hmm! How could you even hope to elude the brilliant Scotland Yard beagles, such as Lestrade and Gregson?'

'Precisely, Doctor! They have a reputation for getting their man.'

Holmes put his fingers together into a steeple and smiled, only just stopping himself from laughing out loud. 'Pray, continue your saga, Mr. Ryder...'

'Thank you, Mr. Holmes. My sister had told me some weeks before that I might have the pick of her geese for a Christmas present, and I knew that she was always as good as her word. I would take my goose now, and in it I would carry my stone to Kilburn. There was a little shed in the yard, and behind this I drove one of the birds, a fine big one, white, with a barred tail. I caught it and, prising its bill open, I thrust the stone down its throat as far as my finger could reach. The bird gave a gulp, and I felt the stone pass along its gullet and down into its crop. But the creature flapped and struggled, and out came my sister to know what all the commotion was. As I turned to speak to her the brute broke loose and fluttered off to mingle with the others.

'"Whatever were you doing with that bird, Jem?"' says she.

'"Well," says I, "you said you'd give me one for Christmas, and I was feeling which was the fattest."'

'"Oh, we have set yours aside for you already. Jem's bird, we call it."'

Blimey – the long, winter nights must have flown by...

'"It's the big white one over yonder. One for you. One for us. Two dozen for the market. That makes twenty-six."'

All the fingers and toes, and six more...

'"Thank you, Maggie," says I; "but if it is all the same to you, I'd rather have that one I was handling just now."'

'"Oh, just as you like," said she, sounding a little huffed. "Which one is it that you want, then?"'

'"That white one..."'

'"They are ALL white, you tease!"

'"The one with the barred tail. I'll take it now."'

'"Very well. Kill it and take it with you."'

'Well, Mr. Holmes, I darned nearly killed myself trying to catch it! But, eventually, I walloped the bird on his head and carried him to Kilburn. I told my pal what I had done, for he was a man that it was easy to tell a thing like that to. He laughed until he choked, and we got a knife and opened the up the goose. My heart turned to water, for there was no sign of the stone, and I knew that some terrible mistake had occurred. I left the bird, rushed back to my sister's, and hurried into the back yard. There was not a bird to be seen there.

'"Where are they all, Maggie?" I cried.'

'"Why they have gone to the dealer. What is it that I do for a living, you muttonhead?!"'

'And, of course, Mr. Ryder,' interjected the great detective, 'it was Breckinridge. Not only that but one of the geese in that consignment was another white gander with a barred tail, almost identical to that which you chose.'

'Yes, apparently so, Mr. Holmes. I ran off as hard as my feet would carry me to this man Breckinridge; but he had sold the lot at once, and not one word would he tell me as to where they had gone. You heard him yourselves tonight. Well, he has always answered me like that. My sister thinks I am going mad. Sometimes I think that myself. And now I find that I am a branded thief, without ever having touched the wealth for which I sold my body and soul. God help me! God help me!'

He burst into convulsive sobbing, with his face buried in his hands. Holmes and I sat back in our chairs and exchanged glances of hope and despair as the shrimp descended into heavy breathing mode. Holmes's face darkened. He dismantled his steeple and started to tap the edge of the table with his fingertips. Then, my friend jumped up suddenly. He marched to the door and threw it open.

'Get out!' said he.

'What, sir! Oh, Heaven bless you!'

'No more blaspheming. Get out!'

And no more blaspheming was offered. The shrimp leaped out of his seat and rushed out of the room. There was a clatter upon the stairs, the bang of the front door, and the crisp rattle of running footfalls could be heard from the street. I looked over to Holmes, who was reaching up his hand for the clay pipe.

'After all, Watson, I am not retained by the police to supply their deficiencies. If Jack Horner were in danger it would be another thing, but this fellow will not appear against him, and the case must collapse. I suppose that I am commuting a felony, but it is just possible that I am saving a soul. This fellow will not go wrong again. He is too terribly frightened. Send him to jail now, and you make him a jailbird for life. Besides, it is the season of forgiveness. Chance has put in our way a most singular and whimsical problem, and its solution is its own reward. If you will have the goodness to touch the bell, Doctor, we will begin another investigation, in which Mrs. Hudson takes the bird from its perch on the Serpentine over there and cooks it for our supper.

A pulled the cord to alert our landlady and rose from my chair.

'I have a little money from a successful Boxing Day's gambling at the Fakenham meet, Holmes. Not much of it left now but I shall go out into Marylebone to find us some claret of a decent vintage.'

'An excellent idea, Watson. Try to fine the Haut Brion '78; it will complement the roasted goose perfectly. Before you go, you had better hand me that small treasure you have picked up from the table and tucked in your right pocket.'

I drew the jewel from my pocket. It was small and beautiful to hold; so smooth and classy; so genuine. I held it up to the light from the fireplace and strained my right peeper. I could see royal blue, and navy blue, dancing in front of my eye and even some deep reds: magenta, damask, crimson and vermilion. Holmes stayed silent, letting me feast my eyes. Then, all of a sudden, I came over all queer, a deeply abnormal feeling that made me feel sick. All of a sudden, I had seen enough. I dropped the gem like a hot coal into his upturned hand.

'There is something deeply disturbing about this stone, Holmes. I'll bet... No, in fact, *I know* that it is more trouble than it is worth.'

'You are absolutely right, Watson. Say farewell to this singularity with a light heart. Ah! Mrs. Hudson!' Our landlady had just entered the room. 'Take this fine goose and roast it for us. We shall dine at seven o'clock!'

If looks could kill!

* * *

And so ended the unique chain of mysterious events that guided us through this extraordinary adventure, one so bizarre that I give you – the faithful – an epitaph.

Holmes insisted on returning the Blue Carbuncle to The Countess of Mordor via Scotland Yard accompanied by some cock-and-bull story about how it had been stolen by a gander, thus exonerating Jack Horner. And that bender, Inspector Gregson, believed him! Isn't it amazing what you can get away with? An unblemished reputation to hide behind, such as that of Mr. Sherlock Holmes?

Gregson insisted that we made a personal delivery to the Countess at her hotel, to slobber and grovel and wax lyrical about what a pleasure it was to provide such a personal service to her ladyship, et cetera. She was so impressed that she gave the reward to the police! Why would *anybody* give £1,000 to the police, I ask you? And the slap in the face was when we were ambushed by a gaggle of journalists on the way into the Hotel Cosmopolitan, with Gregson holding up the Blue Carbuncle in triumph for the photographers, like he had just won the FA cup. We ended up on the front page of *The Telegraph*, which was the start of our road to fame and glory. This, as Mrs. Beeton will tell you, gives the bearer wings on their road to perdition. Holmes was livid! He wanted to know who had tipped off the newshounds, but even the great detective couldn't deduce who the culprit was. Maybe Ryder? Perhaps

Peterson the commissionaire? It might have been Newnes, who would boost circulation of his magazine by making us more familiar to the great British public? Or was it some poor, abused chap who needed to replace his £4. 10/-? I suppose that nobody will ever know who it was.